Contents

Prehistoric Animals
and Fossils

by MICHAEL SMITH, B.A.

with illustrations by ROBERT AYTON

Publishers: Ladybird Books Ltd . Loughborough
© Ladybird Books Ltd 1974
Printed in England

What is a fossil?

For many thousands of years people were puzzled by the strangely-shaped pebbles and patterns inside lumps of rock. Our Stone Age ancestors treasured these because they believed they had magical properties.

Later, some people believed that these oddly-shaped or patterned stones had fallen from heaven. Others thought the Devil had placed them to puzzle mankind, or even that they were the remains of animals that died during Noah's flood.

Many of the markings and patterns certainly looked like parts of familiar plants or animals, but some looked like nothing then living. Also nobody knew why fossils, apparently of sea creatures, were found high in the mountains. The great artist, Leonardo da Vinci (1452–1519), was one of the first to come close to understanding what they were. He thought that they were the remains of animals which had once lived in the sea, that they had been buried in mud and sand which had eventually hardened into rock, and that later this rock had somehow been lifted above sea-level.

Leonardo's ideas, although basically correct, were not widely believed during his lifetime. Only during the last two hundred years have scientists really understood what fossils were and how they were formed.

The word 'fossil' comes from the Latin word *fossilis* (meaning something dug up). At first everything found in the earth was included in the study of fossils, even attractive minerals and the stone tools made by early man. Today the subject is concerned only with the remains or traces of once-living animals and plants.

The elderly Leonardo da Vinci studies a fossil in a rock brought by one of his young admirers.

4

0 7214 0359 X

How a fossil is formed

When an animal dies, its softer parts decay, leaving behind only the hard parts – bones, teeth or shell. If these hard parts are buried by the mud settling on the sea bed, their shapes are often preserved during the millions of years in which the mud is hardening into rock. The original shell or bone may be dissolved away and be replaced, in every detail, by a different substance. Wood or bone keeps its original shape but may be transformed into a hard silica. The shells of sea-snails may be transformed into glistening iron pyrites*, and those of sea-urchins into cream-coloured calcite**.

A buried shell may leave its impression on the mud which settles around it or fills its interior. Although the shell itself may disappear completely, when the rock is split open the pattern revealed can be a perfect replica of the original. The cavity containing such a pattern is known as a 'mould', and the material filling it, a 'cast'.

Occasionally traces of even the soft parts of animals or of delicate leaves are preserved. A thin film of carbon can be left on the surface of some shales‡ or slates, outlining perfectly details of the original shapes.

Because the best conditions for fossilisation are found on the sea floor or in the mud of an estuary, the majority of fossils found are those of animals which once lived in water.

* Iron pyrites – *iron sulphide (a brassy looking mineral, sometimes known as 'fool's gold')*.
** Calcite – *a crystalline form of calcium carbonate*.
‡ Shale – *mud transformed into a thinly-bedded rock which splits easily*.

(above) An ammonite settling on the sea bed 180,000,000 years ago. (Below) Its fossil as found today.

Other kinds of fossils

In prehistoric times, giant reptiles lived near estuaries or swamps where they could find plants to eat and water to drink. When they died their bodies sometimes sank into the mud and their bones eventually fossilised. When these reptiles plodded along the shore, their feet and tails made deep impressions in the sand. If these impressions were baked hard by the sun before more sand or mud was washed over them, they were occasionally preserved. Today, millions of years later, if the rock is split it does so more easily along the surface of such an impression. A series of footprints and impressions can tell us much about the size of the creatures and the way in which they walked.

On rare occasions, the whole of an animal has been preserved intact. Natural lakes of asphalt have trapped large reptiles and sealed their bodies from decay. During the last Ice Age, Woolly Mammoths sometimes fell into deep, snow-filled gullies and were kept in natural refrigeration for thousands of years. A Russian expedition in 1901 'rescued' one specimen from Siberia which is now displayed in a Leningrad museum.

At the other end of the size scale, very small insects were sometimes entombed when settling on the resin oozing down the bark of certain pine trees. The resin hardened into amber, a substance which for centuries has been made into beads and necklaces. Many such beads contain flies and spiders encased in the transparent gum in as perfect condition as on the day they died.

(above) A dinosaur of 150,000,000 years ago.
(below) Dinosaur footprints uncovered in a stone quarry
8 **in Purbeck, Dorset, and now in the British Museum.**

What to look for

Some rocks (such as certain limestones) consist entirely of a mass of shell-like fossils which can be seen easily. In other rocks, however, the fossils may be much further apart, and may differ in colour and texture from the surrounding sediment.

Often only a small portion of a fossil may be visible. Be careful when extracting it from the rock in which it is embedded. Some sandstones and clays are so soft that the fossils can be picked out fairly easily, although care must be taken to avoid damaging delicate shells. In other rocks the fossils may be embedded so solidly that it is almost impossible to extract them. Sometimes a hammer and cold chisel can be used to remove a small block of the rock, from which a specimen can be extracted later.

Occasionally, evidence of a fossil is indicated only by a particular pattern which appears on the surface of a piece of rock which has been split open. Fern leaves and outlines of *trilobites* are fairly common in some shales, and the saw-like markings of *graptolites** can be found on slates.

Types of fossil vary from area to area, and if there is a local museum, you will be able to see from the specimens in the show case what to expect in a particular locality.

* *See page 16*

Some of the fossils you might see.

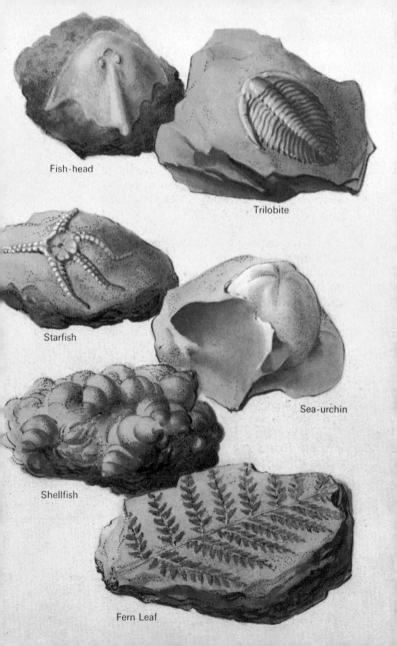

Fish-head

Trilobite

Starfish

Sea-urchin

Shellfish

Fern Leaf

Where to look

Fossils can be found in many of the *sedimentary rocks* exposed over much of Britain. Sedimentary rocks were formed, over many millions of years, as layers and layers of mud and sand were deposited on the sea bed. These layers, or strata, were later forced upwards and may now be seen in cliffs, quarries and cuttings, although sometimes the layers are folded in various directions. Fossils are not found in the large masses of *igneous* rock which formed when molten lava forced its way onto the surface in the form of volcanoes, or solidified just beneath the surface.

Any exposed layer of sedimentary rock is worth examining, but you must *always* ask permission before entering any quarry or pit. Great care must also be taken at the foot of cliffs because of possible rock falls, and because an incoming tide could trap you. Children should *never* try to climb cliffs, *never* go alone *and always* let someone else know exactly where they are going.

You will need a haversack, some newspaper in which to wrap your finds, and a hammer and cold chisel with which to extract pieces of rock containing fossils. Take a notebook and pencil to record what you find and where you found it.

Some fossils are washed out of cliffs and may be found among the pebbles and sand on the beach. Others, particularly of plant remains, may be found on large tips of waste material near coal mines.

Fossil hunting is exciting, takes you out doors and gives enjoyment at home, when you can clean, mount, display and find out more about the specimens you have collected.

The geological map of Britain

The simplified map on pages 48/49 shows where the rocks of the various periods 'outcrop' (come to the surface). Soil, plants or buildings cover them over much of the country. The rocks themselves can be seen only in quarries, cliffs and cuttings, or where slopes are too steep to allow soil to remain on them.

If you compare this map with the relief map in your atlas, you will notice that some hard rocks remain as hills and mountains, while others are much softer and have been worn down to valleys and low plains. Notice how the sedimentary rocks become younger and younger as we travel from the north and west towards the south and east.

At various times in geological history, hot molten magma* forced its way towards the surface, sometimes breaking through to form volcanoes and lava sheets, and sometimes hardening beneath the surface to be revealed much later as the overlying sediments were worn away. These 'igneous' rocks, shown in red, are mainly to be found in Scotland and in the moors of Devon and Cornwall. Because of the way they were formed, these rocks contain no fossils. Great heat and pressure also changed some earlier rocks into *metamorphic* rocks, and if these contained fossils they were usually destroyed, although some badly distorted ones may sometimes be found in slates.

As you will see, most of Britain is formed of sedimentary rocks, in many of which you will be able to hunt for fossils.

* *Magma—the name given to hot molten rock beneath parts of the earth's surface.*

14   **Haytor rocks, Dartmoor, a granite outcrop.**

The Cambrian period – when life existed only in the sea

During the Cambrian period (between five hundred and six hundred million years ago), life existed only in the sea, and the sea floor then looked very different. There was not such a great variety of plant or animal life but we could certainly recognise *some* of the creatures on the sea bed at that time, or which floated gently above the seaweeds.

Transparent jellyfish propelled themselves through the water, their tentacles hanging below parachute-like sacs. As they had no hard parts they have only rarely been found as fossils.

Strange creatures floated like small branches suspended from a transparent balloon. These are called graptolites* because they resemble writing on an old school slate. Their fossils are found in slate and shales. Every branch was a row of tiny, conical cups, each containing a living organism.

An important group of animals we know as trilobites. This word means 'three lobed', because a trilobite could be divided into three distinct sections. As they burrowed into the sea-bottom, or swam just above it, trilobites scavenged for food. The segments of their bodies allowed some of them to curl up like a modern wood-louse if danger threatened. Some were very small indeed, others were as much as eighteen inches long (457 mm). For millions of years they were the most powerful creatures living.

Very well preserved fossils are common in certain areas; one type, *Calymene*, being known as the 'Dudley bug' because it was found so often in quarries near that town.

There were other sea creatures in the Cambrian seas, the ancestors of the sponges, shellfish and sea-urchins.

* *Graptolite—from grapho = I write   lithos = stone*

Jellyfish

Sponges

Trilobites

Other marine life

As time went by, many different types of animal lived in the sea.

Coral is formed by millions of tiny animals which produce skeletons outside their bodies. These lived in the clear, warm, shallow waters and their skeletons piled up to form enormous reefs. Their beautifully patterned skeletons hardened into the rock which we find in some limestone areas. One example is the limestone of Wenlock Edge, in Shropshire, which contains many coral reefs. Many of the different species of coral are divided into radial partitions which look like miniature spokes of a bicycle wheel, but some look just like links in a chain.

Rather similar microscopic animals lived in delicate frameworks, sometimes built onto the shells of other creatures which had just died. Among the commonest of these 'polyzoans' are the lace-like patterns which can be found on the fossilised shells of sea-urchins. A magnifying lens will reveal miniature tubes which also housed the little organisms. Others, again from the Wenlock limestone, look like small branching twigs full of pinpricks. The tiny animals could retract themselves into these tubes when not feeding.

Sponges lived on the sea floor, each extracting food from water drawn in through the countless pores on its surface. Their fossils occur in many shapes and sizes, sometimes even being found in the hollow centres of flints.

Sea-lilies (*crinoids*) swayed in the water, supported by long stems. Tentacles projected from the body and gathered food. Crinoid fossils, particularly broken stems, are so numerous in some limestones that the rock is called 'crinoidal limestone'. Examples are very common in Derbyshire.

A typical Silurian sea bed.

Sea lilies

Sponges

Sponges

Tremacystia (Cretaceous)

Doryderma (Cretaceous)

Sponges

Halysites (Silurian)

Corals

Acervularia (Silurian)

Sea-urchins

Sea-urchins have lived in the seas since Ordovician times (five hundred million years ago), and their fossils are most attractive. The shell (or 'test') is completely surrounded by a mass of spines which help to protect the animal inside. Many years ago, the word 'urchin' meant 'hedgehog' and the term was used because of the obvious resemblance to the friendly creature of the country lane.

When the sea-urchin died, the spines fell away, often to be fossilised separately. The empty, round, disc-like or heart-shaped 'test' filled with sediment, and was eventually replaced by calcite or other materials which kept the beautiful pattern of pores, plates and tubercles of the original. Sometimes silica filled the test or flowed around the outside before hardening into flint. Some patterned pebbles which can be found on beaches near chalk cliffs, must have been formed in this way.

All sea-urchins have a very distinctive five-rayed pattern radiating from the top of the test, and this is clearly recognisable in most sea-urchin fossils. They vary in shape and size, some tests being as big as hockey balls, while others are only the size of marbles. One group is beautifully heart-shaped and named *Micraster* (little star). It is not surprising that country folk call them 'fairy hearts' or 'fairy loaves', and think they bring good luck.

A sea-urchin and some fossils.

A fossil spine

Echinus
(recent)

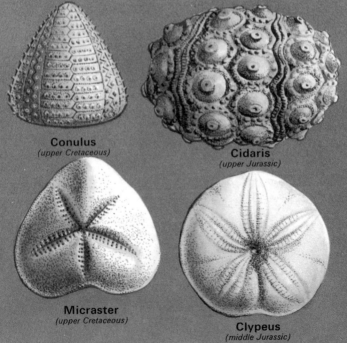

Conulus
(upper Cretaceous)

Cidaris
(upper Jurassic)

Micraster
(upper Cretaceous)

Clypeus
(middle Jurassic)

Fossil shellfish

Among the commonest objects to be found on sea-shores are the shells of animals which have died recently, creatures which had one valve (or shell), or two. On shores in the past there were similar creatures, their valves eventually becoming fossilised. Those with two shells, the bivalves, include the *brachiopods* (lamp shells) and the *lamellibranchs* (oysters, mussels and clams).

The lamp shells, so called because upside-down they look like a Roman lamp, were much more numerous in the past. Most attached themselves to the sea floor by a fleshy stem which came from a small hole in the beak, a hole which can often be seen in the fossil. One valve is usually larger than the other, and in fossil form both valves are often found still joined together. The shells may vary much in shape, size and decoration. As many as thirty thousand different types are known to have lived since their first appearance in the Cambrian seas.

The mollusc bivalves burrowed in sand or mud or fixed themselves to rocks or wood. Most lived in the sea, but some could survive in fresh water. Their fossils also vary in shape, but usually when they died their valves separated and the shells were fossilised singly.

Molluscs having a single shell are known as *gastropods* and include the whelks, snails and limpets. They too lived mostly in water, although some species adapted to life on land. Their coiled, spiral shells are to be found in many different forms and patterns.

Some rocks may be almost completely filled with fossil oysters and snails, the latter in Dorset and Sussex created limestones, sometimes used as polished decorative stonework.

Some examples of fossil shellfish.

Brachiopods

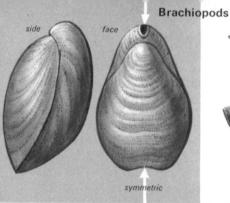

side *face*

symmetric

Lamellibranchs

side *face*

symmetric

Gastropods

Ammonites and belemnites

Having developed from creatures like *Nautilus*, which still survive, *ammonites* and *belemnites* flourished for about three hundred million years before dying out.

The familiar tight coil of a fossil ammonite was once thought to be a snake rolled up and turned to stone by magic. However, we know now that the body of an ammonite was held in the outer chamber of its shell, and was supported by buoyancy tanks which were added as the creature grew. It was able to withdraw into this living chamber and close trapdoors for protection. It could also squirt out a jet of water to enable it to move through the sea. When under attack, it may have produced a cloud of inky fluid to aid its escape.

On falling to the sea bed, the empty, coiled shell became filled with sediment or eventually with pyrites or calcite. These preserved the elaborate decoration and patterns which now help us to identify the many different species.

Ammonites were so named because the coiled form reminded early scientists of the shape of the horns of the god 'Ammon', and the belemnites because their long, pointed shell was dart-shaped – 'belemnon' being the Greek for 'dart'. Belemnites were related to the ammonites, but lived in narrow conical shells which protected their soft bodies. The fossils are often of calcite crystals radiating from the centre of the cone. They can be found in a number of different shapes, some like modern missiles, others more like old-fashioned 'Indian clubs'.

Ammonites and belemnites—the living
creatures and some fossil forms.

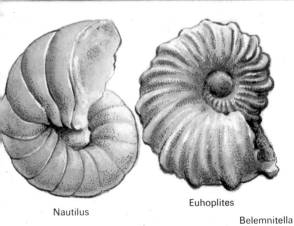

Nautilus   Euhoplites

Belemnitella

Plants begin to cover the Earth

During the Devonian period, (395–345 million years ago) the roots of creeping plants began to spread from the sea into the mud around the mouths of rivers. Warm, damp air and fertile soil made conditions of growth very favourable during the Carboniferous period (350–280 million years ago) when plants such as the horsetails grew in the swamplands. They were like those we see today in marshy patches. Modern horsetails are only two to three feet tall (610–914 mm); those which grew during the Carboniferous period were as high as fifty feet (15 metres).

There were also many kinds of fern. Some pieces of shale, to be found on colliery waste tips, contain fossils of their leaves and show even the pattern of the veins.

Tall trees, very different in appearance from our oaks and pines, thrived in the humid atmosphere. The diamond patterned trunk of *Lepidodendron* supported a branched crown of leaves which must have looked like a giant, green, bursting firework. The straight stem of *Sigillaria* had a neat pattern of leaf scars in orderly vertical rows. The tree, possibly a hundred feet high (30·5 metres), must have looked like an enormous paintbrush.

For millions of years these lush swamp forests were the home of amphibians and myriads of insects. Some of the latter were dragonflies with a wingspan of thirty inches (762 mm).

When the vegetation rotted into thick, peat-like deposits, these were gradually compressed into the layers of coal for which we now find so many uses.

Plants of the Carboniferous swamps.

1. Horse-tails
2. Meganeura *(dragon fly)*
3. Lepidodendron
4. Eryops

Lepidodendron
(Fossilised Bark)

Calamites
(Fossilised Horse-tail)

The earliest fish

Fossils show that fish first appeared in the sea during Silurian times (430–395 million years ago). They looked very different from most we see today. They did not have jaws and were protected by a heavy head shield and armour of bony scales. These we call the *ostracoderms* (bony-skinned). Most were less than one foot (305 mm) long. Another group, the *placoderms* (plate-skinned) had simple jaws and paired fins. Many of these were small, although the *Dinichthys* was thirty feet (9 metres) long, and had jaws powerful enough to crush other fish.

Both groups flourished in the seas of Devonian times, but later the placoderms became extinct and today only the lamprey survives as the one descendant of the jawless fish.

The Devonian period is sometimes called 'The Age of Fishes' because the ancestors of all our modern fish originated then. The commonest fish were those with skeletons made of bone, and bodies covered with slimy scales. Occasionally, the complete impression of such a fish is found, squashed flat, in fossil form, showing every detail of skeleton, scale and fin pattern. More often, however, fossil scales or teeth are found separately and, sometimes, the spines which protruded from the back of the fish.

Primitive sharks also appeared. Their skeletons were not bone, but a softer material called *cartilage*. These sharks had powerful jaws and pointed teeth. Well-preserved fossils of these teeth have been found.

Sharks were as stream-lined as they are today. Many were only a few feet long, but some were even forty feet (12 metres) long. They were so suited to living in the sea that they have prospered ever since.

Palaeozoic fish.

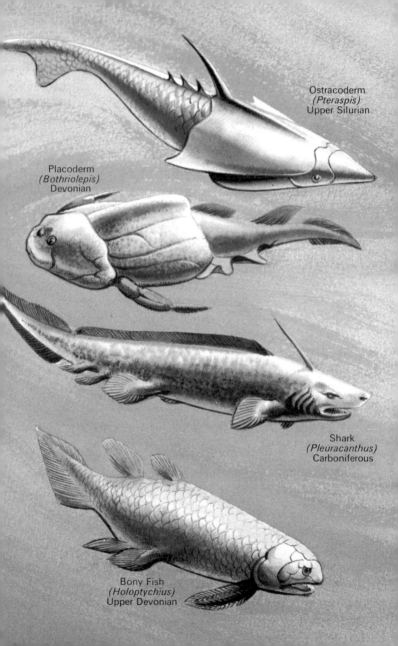

Ostracoderm
(Pteraspis)
Upper Silurian

Placoderm
(Bothriolepis)
Devonian

Shark
(Pleuracanthus)
Carboniferous

Bony Fish
(Holoptychius)
Upper Devonian

Animals begin to move onto the land

Amphibians are creatures which developed from fish, and which can exist in water *and* on land. By the end of the Devonian period, the first amphibians had appeared. They spent most of the time in the water, and had several fish-like features.

The change from living in water to keeping alive on land was difficult to make. A creature living in a river or lake was wholly or partly supported by the water. On land, an animal had to support all its own weight. Therefore its backbone had to become stronger, and its paddles or fins had to develop into limbs capable of moving the body forward. Perhaps the need to change arose because the lakes and swamps began to dry up, making it necessary to seek food on land, or find a way to reach other water.

Even today, surviving amphibians such as frogs and toads lay their eggs in water and the young start life as gill-breathing, swimming creatures. Only later in their life-cycle do they develop lungs and four limbs.

By the end of the Carboniferous period, several species of amphibian dominated the world of swamp and wet forest. Some looked like lizards, others like snakes and crocodiles. Their bodies were protected by an armour of scales or plates.

A. Eryops – 5′ (1.5 metres) long.
B. Diplocaulus – 2′ (610 mm) long.
C. Branchiosaurus – 6″ (152 mm) long.
D. Cardiocephalus – 5″ (127 mm) long.

Reptiles dominate life on land

During the Carboniferous period, the reptiles became the first creatures to develop the ability to lay their eggs and breed on land instead of in the sea. Previous animals had lived chiefly in water, but a change commenced and the reptiles began their domination of life on land, a domination which was to last for nearly one hundred and fifty million years.

Some of the reptiles resembled alligators and turtles. Living in an increasingly dry world, they had to adapt in many ways. Earlier plates and scales were replaced by a horny skin which prevented the loss of too much water.

Dimetrodon, which lived during the Permian period, was a carnivorous animal about ten feet (3 metres) long. It possessed a peculiar sail-like membrane along its back. It is thought that this enabled it to control its body temperature and that by turning side-on to the sun, it could absorb more warmth.

Other adaptations were more frequently made for defensive purposes. *Stegosaurus*, which lived during the Jurassic period (190–140 million years ago), was one of the dinosaurs which developed armour against the attacks of the savage flesh-eaters. It was about twenty to thirty feet (6–9 metres) long and had a double row of thick, bony plates along its back. In the tail were long, sharp spines. It was both slow thinking and slow moving.

(above) Stegosaurus (Jurassic period).
(below) Dimetrodon (Permian period
280–225 million years ago).

The dinosaurs

Many of these early reptiles were very small compared with those grouped together under the name *dinosaur*, which means 'huge reptile'. Undoubtedly dinosaurs arouse the greatest interest. Some must have been quite gentle, clumsy creatures, browsing in swamps and feeding on plants. Others certainly qualified for the description 'terrible', which is often given them, for they were flesh-eating giants of enormous strength and appetite. Perhaps the dinosaur known best is *Brontosaurus*, which, with its close relative, *Diplodocus*, spent much of its life browsing on vegetation in the swamps. Not only did the swamps help to support the heavy weight of these creatures, but there they were safe from the attacks of such fierce monsters as *Tyrannosaurus*, which could not follow them into the water. Brontosaurus was at least sixty-five feet (20 metres) long and weighed about 40 tons (40·641 tonnes).

Tyrannosaurus was probably the most fearsome of the dinosaurs. It was about fifty feet (15 metres) long, twenty feet (6 metres) tall and walked on its hind legs. Having stunted front legs, its power was centred on an enormous jaw set with vicious pointed teeth. It was the largest flesh-eater that has ever lived.

Triceratops was one of the greatest of the armoured dinosaurs. Measuring thirty feet (9 metres) in length, it walked on all four legs and in spite of being a vegetarian was another savage fighter. It relied for defence upon a bony collar which formed a frill behind its neck, and on three horns which stuck out from its face.

(above) Tyrannosaurus attacking Triceratops.
(Cretaceous period)
(centre) Brontosaurus (Jurassic period).
(below) Brontosaurus skeleton.

The end of the dinosaurs

Polacanthus and *Styracosaurus*, shown opposite, were two other kinds of herbivorous (vegetarian) dinosaurs. Only one fossil of the former has ever been found – on the Isle of Wight.

Between 1870 and 1900, fossil hunters in the western states of the U.S.A. uncovered the bones of some very large reptiles. The skeletons which they excavated, or plaster casts of the originals, can now be seen in many museums. It is awe-inspiring to stand dwarfed by the bones of animals which lived more than one hundred million years ago.

It is an astonishing fact that fossils of dinosaur eggs have been found in the Gobi Desert and in France. Bones and teeth found in England show that some types of dinosaur roamed there too, particularly in the area of the Weald.

By the end of the Cretaceous period, these giant reptiles had become extinct after dominating the earth for about one hundred and forty million years. The reasons for this are not fully understood; perhaps future geologists may solve this puzzle. It may be that, as the climate changed and became drier, lakes and swamps dried up so that some of the dinosaurs lost their natural feeding grounds. Other explanations have suggested that they were killed by excessive temperature changes or that mammals learnt to like eating reptile eggs. These possibilities do not account for the fact that the great sea reptiles died out too. But whatever the reason, the dinosaurs disappeared and it was the turn of the mammals to dominate the earth.

(above) Polacanthus (Cretaceous period)
(below) Styracosaurus (Cretaceous period)

Polacanthus

Styracosaurus

The great sea reptiles

Some giant reptiles also lived in the sea. *Ichthyosaurs* (fish-like reptiles) were shaped very much like modern dolphins, being streamlined and having powerful tails and fins which could propel them swiftly through the water. Their shape was much more like that of a fish than the other marine reptiles. They had strong teeth and were able to chase and eat many of the other creatures which swarmed in the sea.

A *plesiosaur* was rather less streamlined, having a fairly bulky body from which a long neck supported a fairly small head. It moved through the water by using flipper-like paddles and, although rather slow, its long snake-like neck was able to move quickly from side to side in order to catch its prey.

When these marine reptiles died, their bodies fell into the mud on the sea floor, and although most must have had their flesh eaten from their bones by other animals, some were covered in sediment before this could happen. The flesh rotted, but an entire skeleton was sometimes preserved. The bones were gradually replaced by a different substance which still preserved every detail of the original. Such skeletons have been found in many Jurassic shales and clays, and may be seen in museums.

Mary Anning, who lived at Lyme Regis, Dorset, during the first half of the nineteenth century, excavated complete specimens which she sold to collectors. Although you may not be as fortunate, it is still possible to find teeth, bone, paddles and vertebrae in old brick pits from which clay has been dug.

The crocodile-like mosasaur in fierce combat with a plesiosaur, while below an ichthyosaur circles warily, awaiting results.

The flying reptiles

During the Jurassic period, some reptiles became able to fly. From their skeletons, it is obvious that they could not have moved through the air as effortlessly as modern birds. The wings of the *pterosaurs* (winged reptiles) were web-like membranes supported by the fore-limbs. Because their wings could not have been flapped vigorously, these reptiles must have relied mostly on air currents to enable them to glide through the air. They probably had to launch themselves from a tree or cliff face.

Flying reptiles varied in shape and size as much as their relatives on land. Some were only the size of a sparrow, while others such as *Pteranodon* which took its food from the sea, had a wingspan of twenty-six feet (8 metres). It was toothless, but many of the other species had jaws crowded with teeth. However, in all the pterosaurs the head was large in comparison with the body. Some types like *Rhamphorhynchus*, had long tails; others such as *pterodactyls* (wing-finger) had much broader wings and only a very short tail.

Beautifully preserved skeletons and outlines have been found in many localities, but the finest are those from the Jurassic 'lithographic limestone' of Bavaria. Here, at Solnhofen, were found also examples of what seems to be a link between the reptiles and the birds. This creature, called *Archaeopteryx** (ancient-wing) was probably the first bird and had evolved feathers from scales, but it also had the reptilian features of a jaw full of tiny pointed teeth, a bony tail and claws on the front of its wings.

* *See cover illustration.*

Pteranodon

Pterodactylus

Rhamphorhynchus

Mammoths of the Ice Age

The Pleistocene Age (which began about one-and-a half million years ago) was one of intense cold. The ice covered vast areas of what is now northern Europe, Asia and America. Around the edges of this ice the ground was frozen and treeless. It was in these areas that herds of Woolly Mammoth roamed in search of food.

During the Middle Ages, numbers of their tusks were found in Siberia and became prized items of trade. No one knew how they got there until scientists discovered that large creatures, similar in appearance to elephants but covered with long hair, were gradually being thawed out of the frozen ground.

After a long and difficult expedition by members of the Russian Academy of Science in St. Petersburg (now Leningrad), one specimen recovered was eventually mounted for display. It had died after breaking its bones by falling into a snow-covered gully. More and more snow which was compressed into ice, completed a 'deep-freeze' process which preserved the mammoth until scientists could study it very many centuries later. From its stomach contents it was even possible to tell that its last meal had been of moss, sedge and pine needles.

Early cave paintings found in France and Spain show very clear pictures of the Woolly Mammoth.

(above) Woolly Mammoth.
(below) Cave painting of a Woolly Mammoth
by Early Man (Dordogne, France).

Your own museum

Once you have found some fossils, you will want to display your best ones. You could prepare small pieces of scrap wood, sandpapered and polished, on which to place single specimens or small groups. Plastic or wooden tops from old containers can support small specimens. Coloured card, or cut polystyrene tiles, provide a background which will show off fossils very well. Your imagination will suggest other kinds of material which can be adapted.

Specimens not on show need to be kept safely. Some hardware shops sell plastic boxes which have partitioned drawers. They fit together, so that more boxes can be added as the collection grows. The names can be written on a card slotted into the front of the box.

However you keep your specimens, it is important that your friends know what they are looking at. Labels can be prepared in neat lettering and each should state the name of the specimen or, if this is not known, the name of the group to which it belongs. Details of each specimen should be recorded in a special notebook or on a card index. Put a reference number on the specimen itself, using Indian ink on a tiny patch of white enamel paint. The notes should include the name of the specimen, exactly where and when it was found, and the type of rock from which it came.

Displaying your collection.

A fossil club

You may have a fossil club at school and be able to use a classroom for meetings or displays. Even if you are unable to do this, it is always possible for a group of enthusiasts to meet and discuss their finds.

Any group of fossil hunters will naturally want to go out together on collecting expeditions. Each member will probably have his or her own favourite spot to which to take the group. It is also useful to hold regular meetings so that specimens can be prepared for study or exhibition. Perhaps an expert might be invited to talk to the club about certain types of fossils or about life in the geological past. Many museums welcome a group visit, and may even arrange a special programme.

The artists in a group could paint pictures representing plant and animal life of the particular periods from which the members have collected specimens – the details being found from books such as this. Models of prehistoric animals could be made from wire and papier mâché or from plastic kits available from toy shops. If placed in front of paintings, these add a third dimension to a display. Photographers in the group could make a valuable record of the location of the local rocks which contain fossils. Someone with a tape recorder could perhaps produce a documentary programme about fossils or a commentary about life in one of the geological periods.

Your group might get in touch with similar clubs in different parts of the country, so that you can learn about fossils available to them or perhaps even exchange spare specimens.

(above) Preparing a display model.
(below) A finished exhibit.

BRONTOSAURUS

A herbivorous creature that lived in swampy lakes. It could grow 70 feet long. In spite of its great size it weighed only a few tons.

A generalised geological map of Britain

Quaternary drift

Tertiary rock

Cretaceous rock

Jurassic rock

Triassic and Permian rock

Coal fields

Lower Carboniferous to Cambrian rock

Igneous and Metamorphic rock

The geological time-scale

The Earth came into being about 4,500 million years ago. Little is known about any life on Earth during the first 4,000 million years. It is from the fossilised remains in the Cambrian rocks (formed 500–600 million years ago), and in the rocks which were formed afterwards, that geologists have reconstructed the story of 600 million years of plant and animal life on earth. The rock layers unfold the story as clearly as the pages of a history book tell the events of the last thousand years.

Geologists have divided up, like the chapters of a book, this enormous length of time into four sections. These are referred to as 'Primary', 'Secondary', 'Tertiary' and 'Quaternary', meaning simply 'first', 'second', 'third' and 'fourth'. Because fossils show important changes in the life of these 'eras', the first three are sometimes named 'Palaeozoic' (ancient life), 'Mesozoic' (middle life) and 'Cainozoic' (new life).

Each era is further split into periods. These periods were given names often referring to an area in which the rocks of that period were first studied by the early geologists. So 'Cambrian' rocks were named after Cambria – the old word for Wales, where examples of these particular rocks are situated. The Ordovician and Silurian periods are named after rocks found in regions once occupied by tribes of these names. The Devonian period is named after the type of rocks found in Devon.

The origins of the names of the remainder of the periods you can see on the time-scale opposite, which also tells you how to pronounce them. You can also see how long each period lasted.

ERA	PERIOD	Years in millions		MEANING
		Time span	How long ago	
Quaternary	HOLOCENE	1	1	Referring to shells similar to types alive in our seas today
	PLEISTOCENE	1	2	
Tertiary (Cainozoic) Kane-o-zo-ic	PLIOCENE	13	15	
	MIOCENE	20	35	
	OLIGOCENE	10	45	
	EOCENE	25	70	
Secondary (Mesozoic) Me-so-zo-ic	CRETACEOUS Kret-eh-shous	70	140	Creta (Latin) = chalk
	JURASSIC Jur-as-sic	50	190	named after the Jura mountains
	TRIASSIC Tri-as-sic	35	225	meaning 3 divisions
Primary (Palaeozoic) Pal-eh-o-zo-ic	PERMIAN Per-me-an	55	280	named after Perm in the Ural mountains
	CARBONIFEROUS	65	345	coal bearing
	DEVONIAN	50	395	named after Devon
	SILURIAN Cy-lur-e-an	35	430	named after the tribe Silures
	ORDOVICIAN Ord-o-vish-e-an	70	500	named after the ancient British tribe - the 'Ordovices'
	CAMBRIAN Cam-brie-an	70	570	named after Cambria - the old name for Wales
	PRE-CAMBRIAN	?	4500	as above

Classification of common fossi

Phylum	Important representatives		
PROTOZOA	*Single-celled animals (MICROSCOPIC*		
PORIFERA	*Sponges*		
COELENTERATA	*Corals*		
POLYZOA	*Lace polyzoan*	*Stick polyzoa.*	
BRACHIOPODA	*Bivalve (lamp shells)*		
MOLLUSCA	*Cephalopods*	*Ammonites*	
		Belemnites	
	Lamellibranchs	*(Bivalves)*	
	Gastropods	*(Single-valve)*	
ECHINODERMATA	*Starfish*		*Rar*
	Echinoids (sea-urchins)		
	Crinoids (sea-lilies)		
ARTHROPODA	*Crustacea*		
	Trilobites		
CHORDATA	*Graptolites*		
	Fish		
	Amphibia		
	Reptiles		
	Mammals		
	Birds		